Grimm's Fairy Tales

For Auntie Louise
S.P.

For Aunt Marie
C.J.

ORCHARD BOOKS
338 Euston Road, London NW1 3BH
Orchard Books Australia
Level 17/207 Kent Street, Sydney, NSW 2000

This text was first published in the form of a gift collection called
The Sleeping Princess by Orchard Books in 2002

This edition first published in hardback in 2012
First paperback publication in 2013

ISBN 978 1 40830 843 1 (hardback)
ISBN 978 1 40830 844 8 (paperback)

Text © Saviour Pirotta 2002
Illustrations © Cecilia Johansson 2012

The rights of Saviour Pirotta to be identified as the author and
Cecilia Johansson to be identified as the illustrator of this work
have been asserted by them in accordance
with the Copyright, Designs and Patents Act, 1988.

A CIP catalogue record for this book is available

ry.

back)
·back)

e Children's Books,
.ny.

Grimm's Fairy Tales

Twelve Dancing Princesses

Written by Saviour Pirotta
Illustrated by Cecilia Johansson

ORCHARD

Once there was a king who had twelve
beautiful daughters. They all liked dancing!
So the king locked them all in one big
bedroom at night, in case they tried to sneak
out to a ball or party.

One morning, when the king unlocked the door, he saw that the princesses' satin shoes had been danced to pieces.

"Did you find a way out of your room?"
the king asked his daughters. The princesses
wouldn't say anything, no matter how much
he thundered and pleaded. And no one else in
the palace had seen them creeping out either.
It was all a big mystery.

The same thing happened the next night . . .

. . . and the night after that.

The king was very upset and worried. He sent out a proclamation, inviting all the young men of the land to discover the princesses' secret.

Any prince who found out the secret could choose one of the king's daughters to marry and would inherit the kingdom. But any prince who tried and failed three nights in a row would lose his head.

Many a dashing young prince accepted the challenge. In turn, each was given a sumptuous supper and at bedtime was shown to a chamber next to the princesses' bedroom.

But every prince fell asleep at his task and every morning the king found the princesses' shoes tattered and torn.

Many princes lost their lives and the princesses' secret remained just that: a secret.

It so happened that a tired soldier found himself in the city. By chance he met a kind old woman who, seeing the weariness in his face, asked him where he was going.

"I'm not sure," he replied. "I might try and discover where the king's daughters dance at night."

"In that case," said the woman, who was really a kind witch, "do not drink the wine that the princesses offer you, because it has a sleeping potion in it.

"And, when they go out, put on this cloak to make you invisible, and follow them."

The soldier thanked the old woman and hurried to the palace.

That night, the soldier pretended to drink the goblet of wine but actually emptied it into the chamberpot under the bed.

Then he lay down, yawned and began to snore loudly, pretending to be asleep.

In the big room next door, the twelve princesses put on their silk party dresses and satin dancing shoes. Then the eldest daughter knocked on one of the beds and it sank into the floor, revealing a secret staircase.

The princesses descended through the opening, one after another.

The soldier put on his magic cloak and quickly followed them.

At the bottom of the stairs was a garden full of silvery trees. The soldier, unable to help himself, reached out and snapped off a twig.

"Did you hear that noise?" asked the youngest princess.

"It was nothing," scolded the eldest princess.

She led the way into a second garden,
where the trees were made of gold . . .

. . . and then to a third garden, where the
trees had diamonds instead of fruit.

In each garden, the soldier broke off a twig.

At last the princesses reached the shores of a lake. There, twelve handsome princes were waiting, each one sitting in a boat. Across the lake, a palace stood on the hill.

Every princess got into a boat . . .

. . . and the invisible soldier hopped in with the youngest and her prince.

Soon, all twelve boats were moored outside the palace, and the twelve princesses were dancing inside.

By sunrise the princesses' shoes were worn to shreds.

The princes rowed the tired princesses across the lake. "We'll come back tomorrow," said the princesses.

When they got to the secret passage, the soldier hurried on ahead, took off his invisible cloak and jumped into bed.

The next night, the soldier followed the princesses again. And the night after that! On the fourth night, the soldier stole a wine goblet from the ballroom.

At last it was time for the soldier to be summoned before the king.

"I have solved the mystery, Your Majesty," said the soldier.

"Every night, your daughters escape through a secret tunnel to a palace on the shores of an underground lake. There they dance with twelve handsome princes."

He showed the king the silver, gold and diamond twigs and gave him the wine goblet.

The king called for the princesses at once and, seeing the evidence before them, they confessed to their secret.

The king asked the soldier to choose one of the princesses as his bride. He took the eldest, because she had a mischievous smile and was the closest to him in age.

The wedding was held that very same day, with much feasting. Everyone at the party danced until their shoes had fallen to pieces.